THE GREAT CHANGE

Text by White Deer of Autumn • Illustrations by Carol Grigg • Beyond Words Publishing, Inc.

Published by
Beyond Words Publishing, Inc.
13950 NW Pumpkin Ridge Road
Hillsboro, Oregon 97123
Phone: 503 647 5109
Toll-free: 1 800 284 9673

Design: Principia Graphica

Printed in Mexico.
Distributed by Publishers Group West.

Library of Congress Cataloging-in-Publication Data

White Deer of Autumn
    The great change / written by White Deer of
Autumn ; illustrated by Carol Grigg.
        p. cm.
    Summary: A Native American grandmother
explains the meaning of death, or the Great Change,
to her questioning granddaughter.
    ISBN 0-941831-79-5 : $13.95
    [1. Death – Fiction. 2. Indians of North America –
Fiction.]
I. Grigg, Carol, 1942-   . ill.   II. Title
PZ7.W58495Gr 1992   92-14501
[Fic]–dc20   CIP
                                          AC

For Dora Davis and all the Grandmothers who
have poured their cups of goodness back for
future generations.

White Deer of Autumn

This book is dedicated to the children of all
nations who are sharing their diversity and
keeping the world circle strong.

Carol Grigg

The aged Indian woman and her granddaughter pulled the fish they had netted onto the shore. Back and forth they went to the sea, returning the fish they did not need. Those remaining in their net jumped and flipped about until they lay still.

In her nine years of life, death of any kind had seemed distant to Wanba. But that was before Grandpa died. Now, watching the silver scales shimmer in the baking sun, she wished even more that death didn't have to be at all.

Quickly Grandma began the task of carefully scraping and cutting the fish. "Best to put what remains of them in here, my girl," she said, reaching for a sack. "I'll carry what we can eat in mine."

As they tied their sacks with twine, the old one paused. Lifting her calico skirt, she wiped beads of sweat from her face while Wanba's eyes followed a trail of great birds. With wings spread wide, they sailed the wind currents, swooping in long, high arcs.

"Look, Grandma, pelicans!"

The great birds circled, searching for the bright streaks flashing near the surface. Suddenly, they rose straight up. Their necks craned, and their eyes fixed downward. Swiftly and deadly, they dove like feathered spears dropping from the sky.

"Grandma! Grandma!" she cried.

Listening to the splashing pelicans and gathering gulls, Grandma lifted her catch and stood tall. A quick gust of salty air lifted her silver braids and pulled them back. They waved in the wind like the fronds of the sabal palms that lined the forest behind her.

"It is a time of Great Change," she said. "Now the fish become the food of life."

Wanba gazed down at her sack still on the sand. Her fingers fidgeted with the twine. The gust calmed.

"Grandma, why do the fish have to die? Why does anything have to die? Can't things just live?" She kicked the sand with her toes. Death was something she couldn't understand.

The old one watched the pelicans quietly float, digesting their meal.

"So the Circle of Life is never broken," she answered.

"You see, my girl, the pelicans, like all things, live within the Circle of Life. And like us, they take only what they need. We need death in order to have life."

"But why did Grandpa have to die?"

Grandma searched the rippling water for other signs that could help her answer, but there were none. Suddenly the memory of her husband made her feel empty.

"We should go now," she said, hoping the signs would come as they always had.

And until they did, Wanba would have to wait.

Down the beach, over the dunes, and onto the trail winding through the forest they walked. At times, feelings and memories blurred the trail ahead of the old one, but they seemed to excite Wanba.

"Remember how Grandpa used to carry me most of the way home, Grandma?"

"Yes," she smiled, "when you were little. Now you can walk all the way, and I'm getting too old."

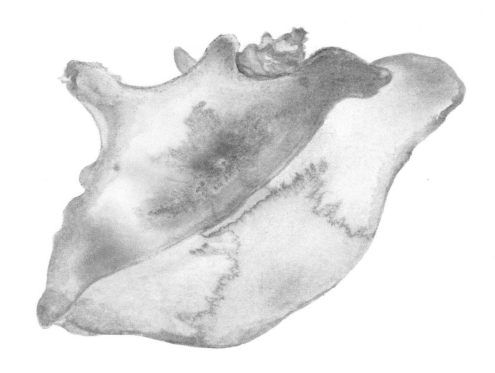

Just off the trail, they
entered a circle of palms
and sat on a log to rest.
This was Grandma's special
place. Surely, the old one
thought, if a sign were to
come, it would be here.

As Wanba picked at the dark, gray wood, a small caterpillar crawled onto Grandma's hand. All those tiny legs tickled her soft skin.

It was the sign Grandma needed.

"Look!" she laughed. "This is a butterfly before she becomes one."

Wanba gently stroked the fuzzy creature with her finger.

"You see, my girl, she goes about close to Mother Earth, getting to know even the tiniest things."

"Sort of like me, Grandma?"

"Indeed," the old one grinned, "sort of like you. And when she is old enough, she'll spin a cocoon and go into a deep sleep. When she wakes up, she'll have wings! Then she'll fly away, bringing more beauty into this world, just like you will."

"But, Grandma, what happens to the caterpillar? Does she die?"

"No, she changes into the butterfly. Nothing stays the same, my girl. All things change."

Grandma put the insect down. "But one day," she continued, "the butterfly will tire of flying. The nights will grow too cold for her, and her life as a butterfly will end. At that time, she will return to Mother Earth and nourish new life. That's when she dies. But all dying means, Wanba, is *change*."

She patted her granddaughter's knee and rose. "Time to go," she said. And the two lifted their sacks and left the circle of palms.

Near their home, they reached the garden of the old ones and stopped by a row of young corn.

"Let's dig around these plants, my girl. If they're to feed us, we'd best care for them."

Like the older stalks at the edge of the garden bending from the long summer, the old one leaned down with great effort and marked where the holes were to go. Then, sitting on the warm earth, she asked Wanba to untie her sack. Strands of the old woman's silver hair twirled like corn tassels as her cracked and wrinkled hands dug and lifted the dirt. Wanba knelt close to help, startled at how much Grandma's hands looked like the earth.

"Empty some of your sack here, my girl. We'll return to Mother Earth the fish parts we do not eat. Then she will nourish the young corn and help them grow."

"Grandma, is this what happened to Grandpa? Did he return to the earth like the fish?"

The old woman pushed the sandy dirt back into the hole, remembering that wintry day she gave Grandpa back to the land. "His body did, Grandchild. Like the fish, and someday like the butterfly too, he is one with Mother Earth again."

Grandma stood slowly, her voice rising in a warm gust. "But the 'special part' of Grandpa became part of everything that lives, my girl!"

As they left the garden that summer afternoon, they felt Grandpa all around. Everywhere they looked, the gentle strength of the land reminded them of him.

Just before the two reached the small frame house where Wanba's grandparents had lived for forty years and Wanba had lived for every summer of her life, they stopped. At the edge of a dark, spring-fed pond was the well where Grandma drew her water. Alongside the pump they began to wash their catch of fish.

"Grandma, I know what happened to Grandpa's body after his . . . Great Change. But what is the 'special part' of Grandpa?"

The old one stopped pumping. "That's a hard question, Wanba."

She picked up an old copper cup and held it, thinking while they sat together at the rim of the spring pond.

"Some people call the 'special part' that gives life to things *spirit*. Some call it *soul*. Others say *God*. Our ancestors called it the *Great Mystery*."

Grandma reached down and scooped up some water, filling the cup.

"Let's say this little pond is the Great Mystery that gives life to things. If you take a cup for your life, my girl, and I take one for mine, and everything everywhere takes one, there would be no more water. Then what would happen?"

"Nothing new could be born, Grandma. There would be nothing left."

"Right.

"And," she continued, "as you live your life you try to fill your cup with Good. Then, when it's time for you to make the Great Change, all that Good will pour back into the Mystery with Grandpa's and mine."

Wanba watched her grandmother empty the cup into the pond, forming rings that grew away. "And the Circle of Life is never broken," she murmured.

The old one nodded.

"Will we ever see Grandpa again?"

"Close your eyes and remember him, my girl. See him on the backs of your eyelids!"

Wanba shut them tight for a few moments. "I . . . I can see him, Grandma," she whispered. A warm breeze surrounded her. "I can feel him too," she sighed.

The old woman brushed back the black silky strands of her granddaughter's hair. "There is no death in the Circle of Life," she said, "only the Great Change."

That night after supper, while an old lantern flickered shadows on the wall, Wanba got into bed. Grandma sat on the edge. She leaned down, and with her lips close to Wanba's ear, she asked softly, "Are you all right?"

"Grandma, what does my name mean? It's . . . different than the other kids at my school."

"My grandmother wanted you to carry her name, my girl. She told me that the old language would live on in your name. It means *wandering beam*. She said that if you painted it, you'd have a butterfly in a bright, misty cloud."

Wanba scooched down under her star-quilt. "This is sort of like a cocoon, isn't it, Grandma?"

"A cocoon of stars, little Wandering Beam. Now, close your eyes and sleep. Think of the wonderful summer we have left together. Like the caterpillar who dreams of becoming a butterfly, dream of your own changing." Wanba felt the old lips brush her cheek.

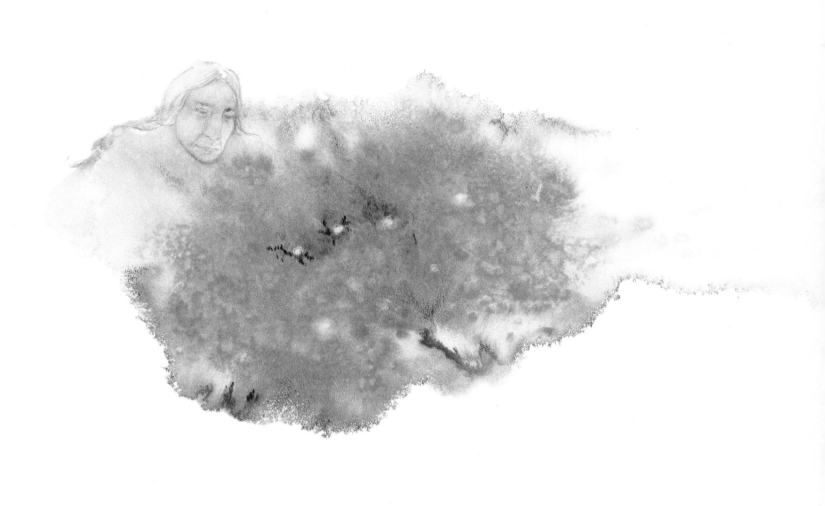

Grandma rose, her shoulders bent slightly, and reached for the lantern. In two breaths she blew it out. Her moccasined feet made a shuffling sound as she stepped to the door and opened it.

Gazing up at the black sky, she saw Grandpa in the silver stars. Within her old body, she sensed her own 'special part' stirring restlessly and knew it would be soon that her goodness would join his in the Great Mystery—and in Wanba. And she knew that the Circle of Life would remain for another generation—unbroken and strong.

OTHER NATIVE AMERICAN CHILDREN'S BOOKS
FROM BEYOND WORDS PUBLISHING, INC.

THE NATIVE AMERICAN BOOK OF KNOWLEDGE

Author: White Deer of Autumn. Illustrator: Shonto Begay

Investigates the fascinating and controversial origins of the People, based on tales from various tribes, scientific evidence, and archaeological finds. Discusses several key figures in the Americas, including Deganawida, Hyonwatha, and others who have had a mystical and spiritual impact on the Native people. 96 pages, $4.95 softbound, ages 10 and up.

THE NATIVE AMERICAN BOOK OF LIFE

Author: White Deer of Autumn. Illustrator: Shonto Begay

Speaks of the great importance of children in the Native way of life; about their pastimes, how they are named, initiated into everyday society, taught, disciplined, and cared for. A fictional, magical story about children visiting a Native museum and learning about the many practices relating to food and the People: food growing and gathering practices, feasting traditions, and food contributions. 96 pages, $4.95 softbound, ages 10 and up.

THE NATIVE AMERICAN BOOK OF CHANGE

Author: White Deer of Autumn. Illustrator: Shonto Begay

Common stereotypes of Native Americans are explored and debunked, while passing on our personal "shields" — positive points of view that tell ourselves and others who and what we are — is encouraged. An important look back in time that focuses on the People's interaction with whites: the conquests of the Toltec, Aztec, Mayan, and North American tribes are covered. 96 pages, $4.95 softbound, ages 10 and up.

THE NATIVE AMERICAN BOOK OF WISDOM

Author: White Deer of Autumn. Illustrator: Shonto Begay

Explores the fascinating belief system of the People, from the concept of the Great Mystery, or Wakan-Tanka, to the belief that all life is sacred and interrelated. A tribal medicine man visits a contemporary classroom and the children are amazed at what he has to tell them about the traditions and power of his people. 96 pages, $4.95 softbound, ages 10 and up.

CEREMONY IN THE CIRCLE OF LIFE

Author: White Deer of Autumn. Illustrator: Daniel San Souci

The story of nine-year-old Little Turtle, a young Native American boy growing up in the city without knowledge of his ancestors' beliefs. He is visited by Star Spirit, who introduces him to his heritage and his relationship to all things in the Circle of Life. Little Turtle also learns about nature and how he can help to heal the Earth. 32 pages, $6.95 softbound, $14.95 hardbound, ages 6-10.